Dr. Seuss' CLEVER CREATURES

HarperCollins *Children's Books*

Dr. Seuss' Clever Creatures

An omnibus edition adapted from Horton Hears a Who!, Yertle the Turtle and Other Stories and Thidwick the Big-Hearted Moose.

First published in the UK by HarperCollins Children's Books in 2008

1 3 5 7 9 10 8 6 4 2

ISBN-10: 0-00-728457-8

ISBN-13: 978-0-00-728457-3

A CIP catalogue record for this title is available from the British Library.

www.harpercollinschildrensbooks.co.uk

Horton Hears a Who!

First published in the UK in 1976

Yertle the Turtle and Other Stories

 First published in the UK in 1963

Thidwick the Big-Hearted Moose

First published in the UK in 1968

Printed and bound in Hong Kong

HORTON HEARS A WHO!

By

Dr. Seuss

HarperCollins *Children's Books*

For My Great Friend,
Mitsugi Nakamura
of Kyoto,
Japan.

On the fifteenth of May, in the Jungle of Nool,
In the heat of the day, in the cool of the pool,
He was splashing . . . enjoying the jungle's great joys . . .
When Horton the elephant heard a small noise.

So Horton stopped splashing. He looked towards the sound.
"That's funny," thought Horton. "There's no one around."
Then he heard it again! Just a very faint yelp
As if some tiny person were calling for help.
"I'll help you," said Horton. "But *who* are you? *Where?*"
He looked and he looked. He could see nothing there
But a small speck of dust blowing past through the air.

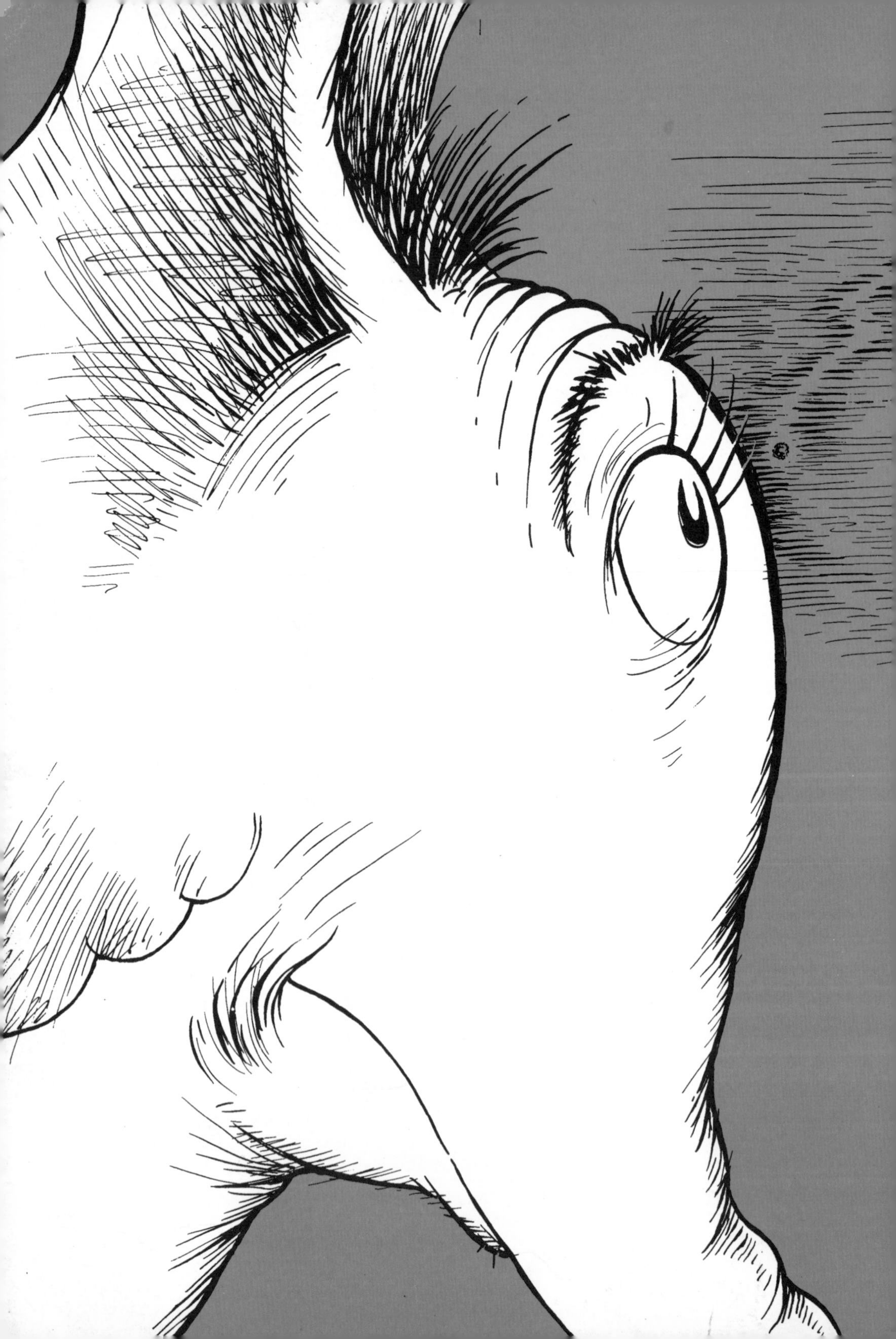

"I say!" murmured Horton. "I've never heard tell
Of a small speck of dust that is able to yell.
So you know what I think? . . . Why, I think that there must
Be someone on top of that small speck of dust!
Some sort of a creature of *very* small size,
Too small to be seen by an elephant's eyes. . .

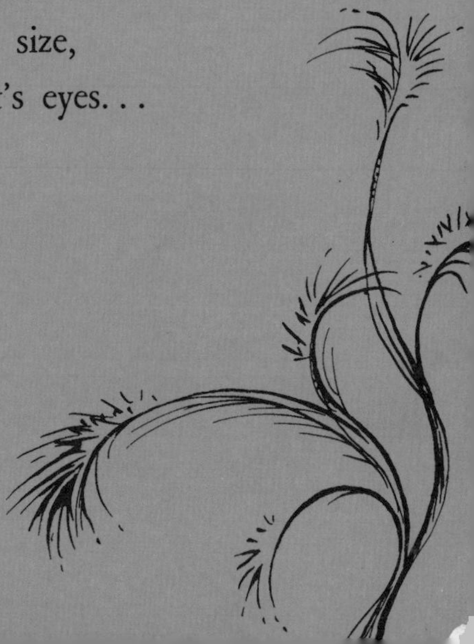

"...some poor little person who's shaking with fear
That he'll blow in the pool! He has no way to steer!
I'll just have to save him. Because, after all,
A person's a person, no matter how small."

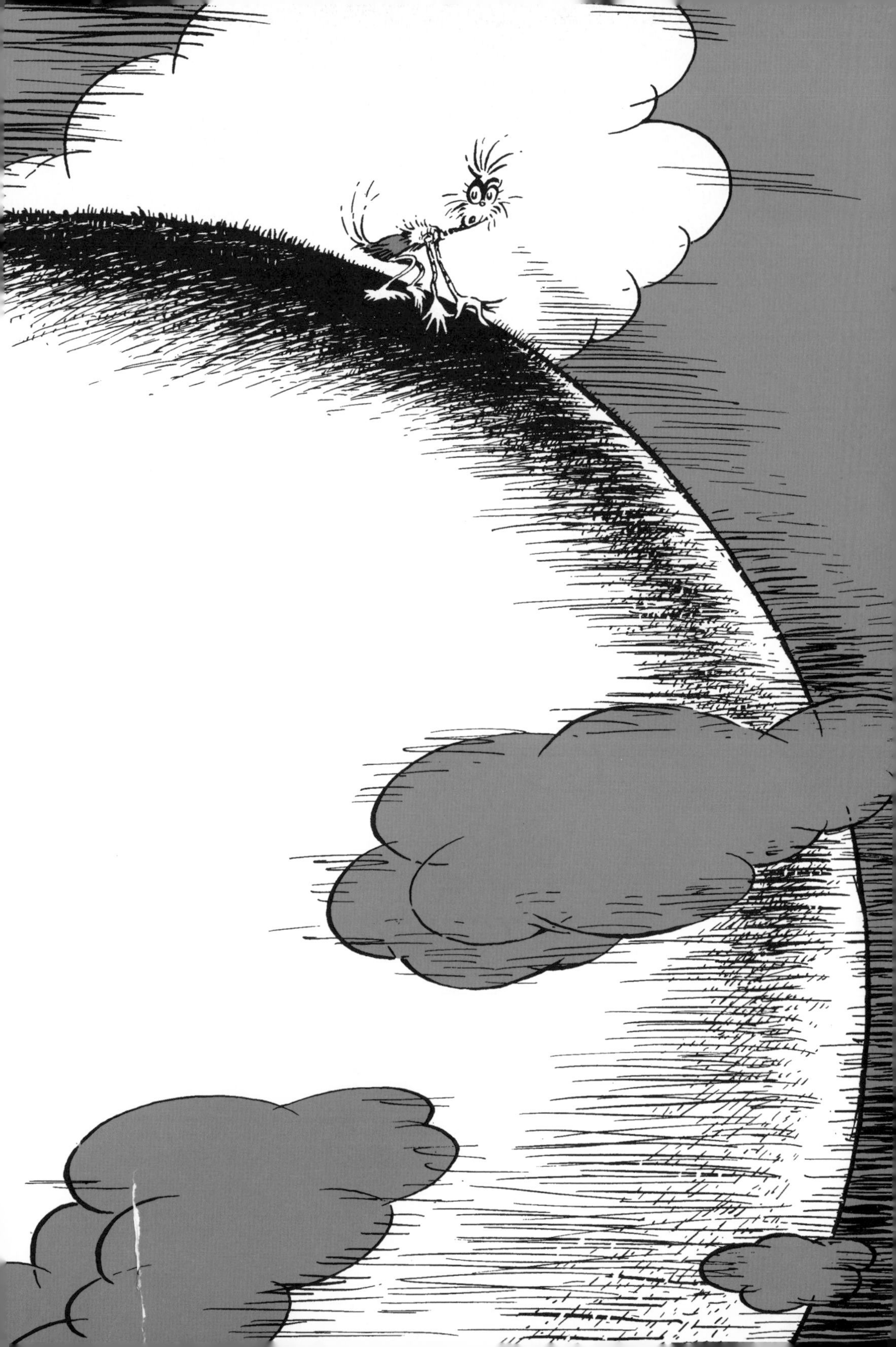

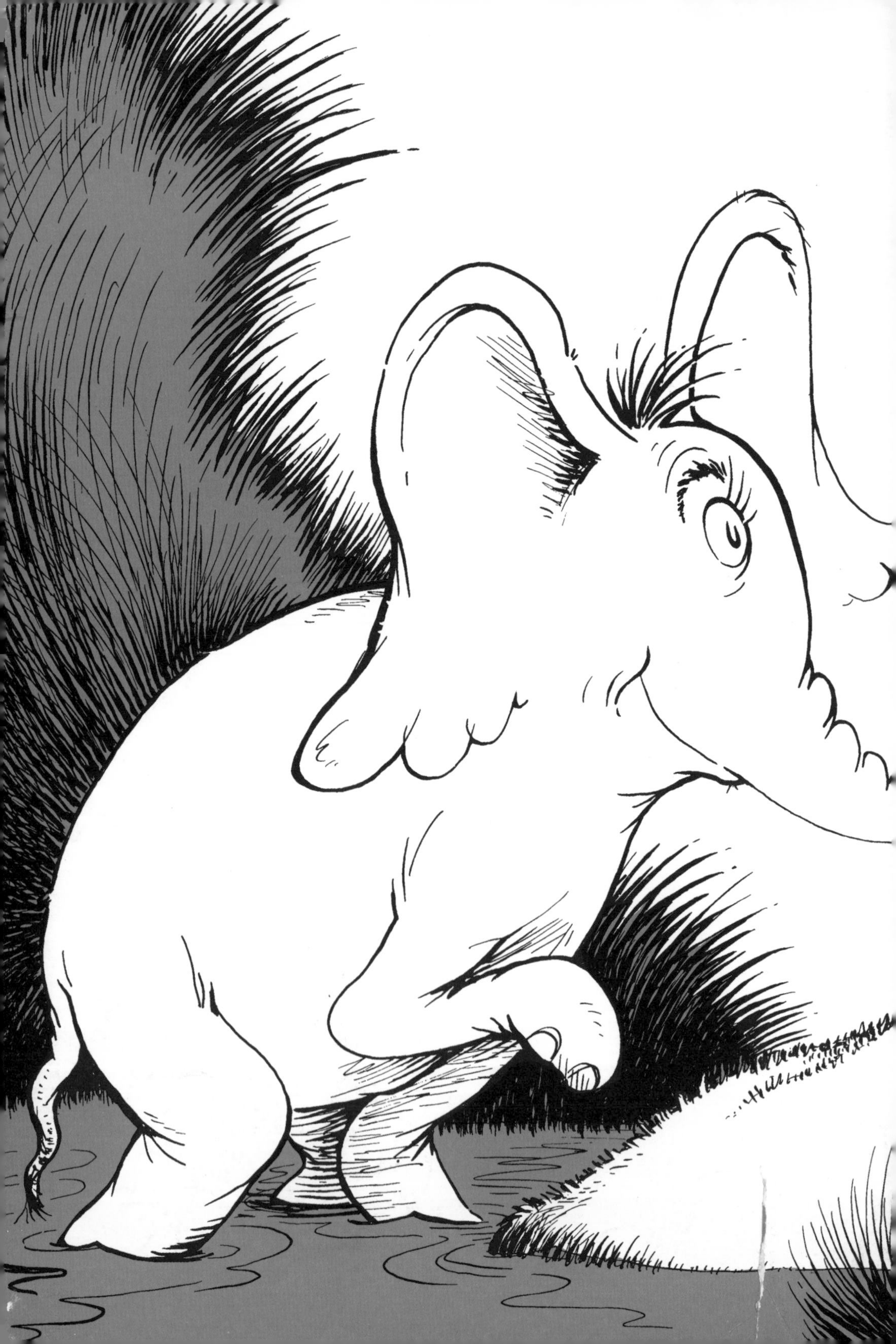

So, gently, and using the greatest of care,
The elephant stretched his great trunk through the air,
And he lifted the dust speck and carried it over
And placed it down, safe, on a very soft clover.

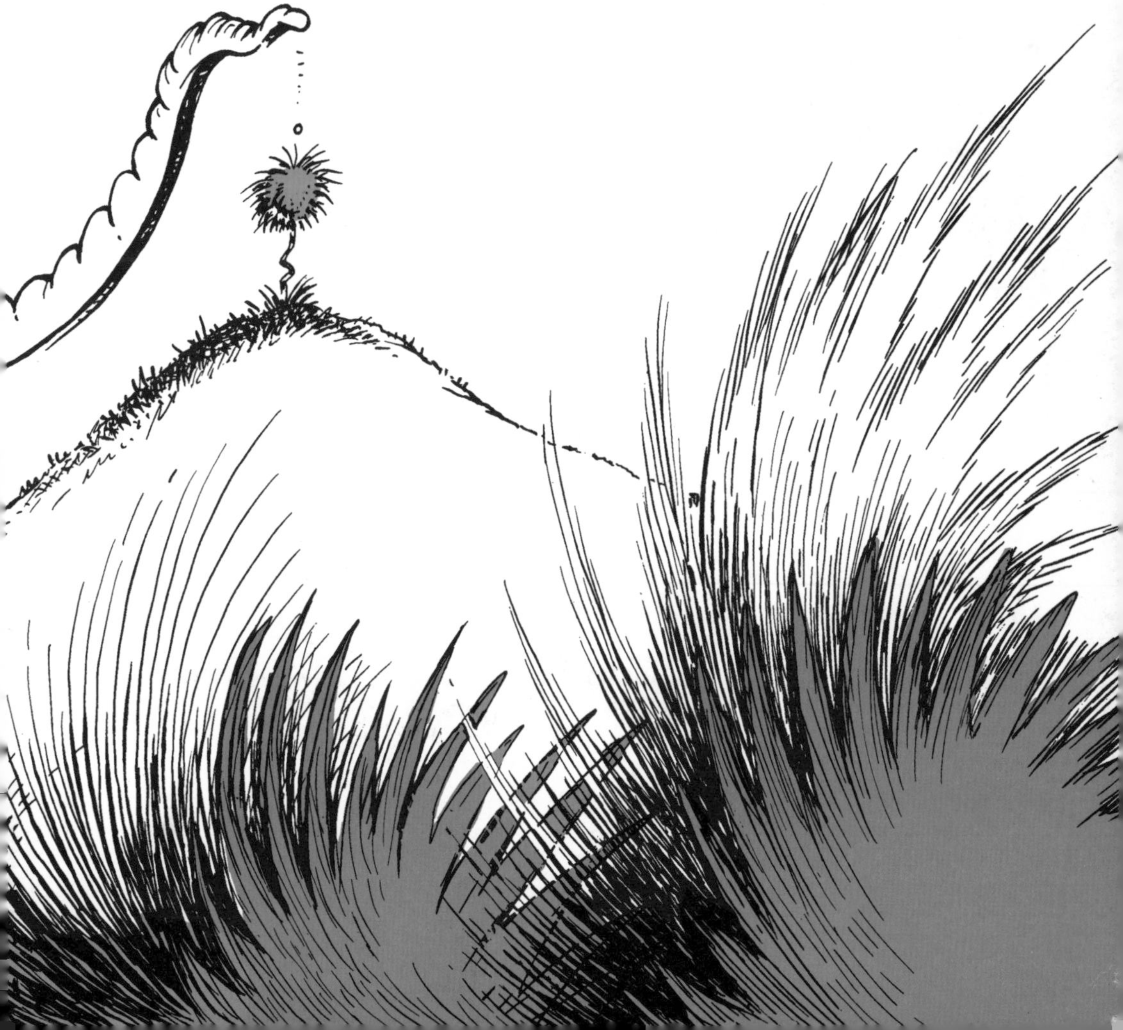

"Humpf!" humpfed a voice. 'Twas a sour kangaroo.
And the young kangaroo in her pouch said "Humpf!" too
"Why, that speck is as small as the head of a pin.
A person on *that?* . . . Why, there never has been!"

"Believe me," said Horton. "I tell you sincerely,
My ears are quite keen and I heard him quite clearly.
I *know* there's a person down there. And, what's more,
Quite likely there's two. Even three. Even four.
Quite likely . . .

". . . a family, for all that we know!
A family with children just starting to grow.
So, please," Horton said, "as a favour to me,
Try not to disturb them. Just please let them be."

"I think you're a fool!" laughed the sour kangaroo
And the young kangaroo in her pouch said, "Me, too!
You're the biggest blame fool in the Jungle of Nool!"
And the kangaroos plunged in the cool of the pool.
"What terrible splashing!" the elephant frowned.
"I can't let my very small persons get drowned!
I've *got* to protect them. I'm bigger than they."
So he plucked up the clover and hustled away.

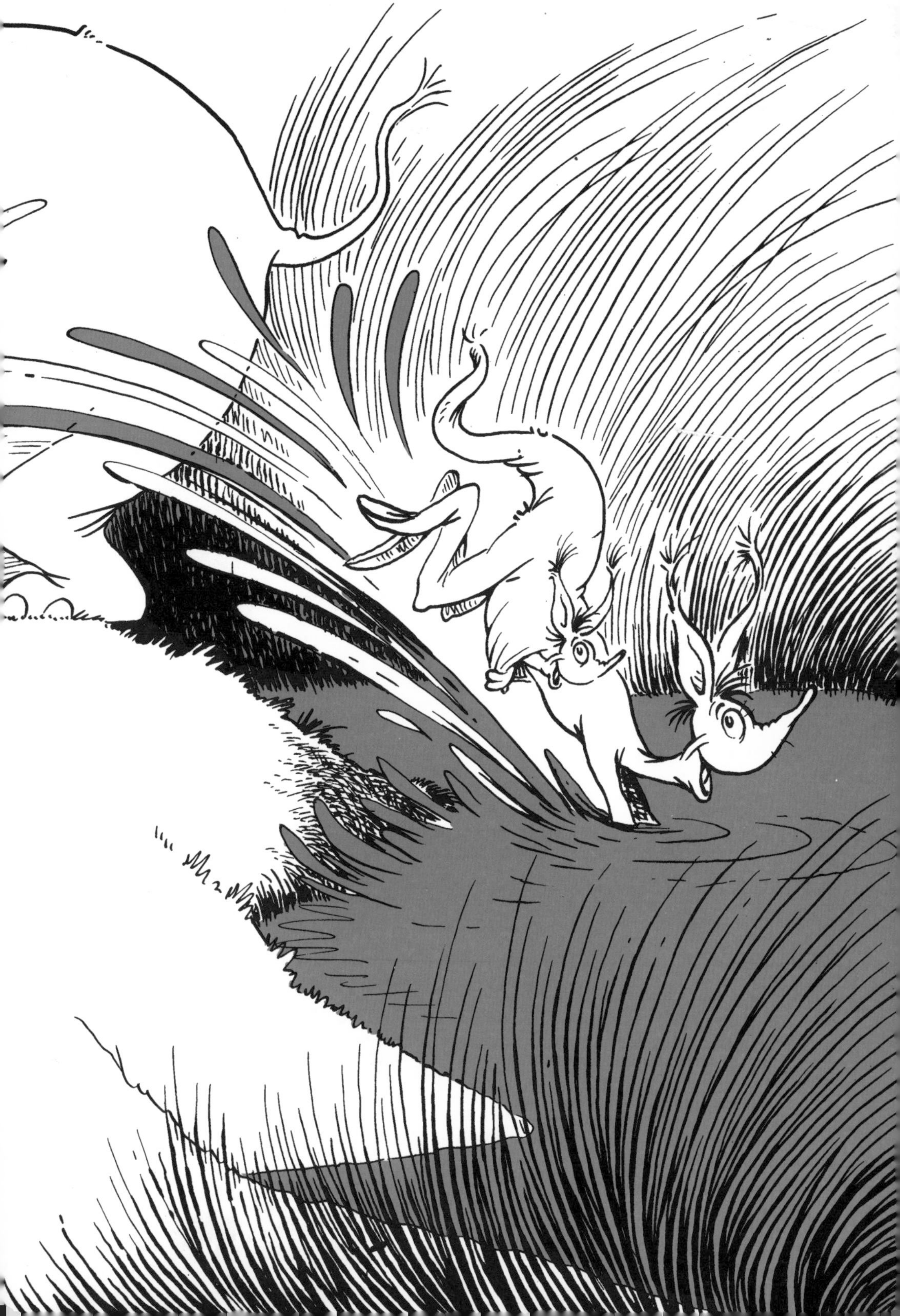

Through the high jungle tree tops, the news quickly spread:
"He talks to a dust speck! He's out of his head!
Just look at him walk with that speck on that flower!"
And Horton walked, worrying, almost an hour.
"Should I put this speck down? . . ." Horton thought with alarm.
"If I do, these small persons may come to great harm.
I *can't* put it down. And I *won't!* After all
A person's a person. No matter how small."

Then Horton stopped walking.
The speck-voice was talking!
The voice was so faint he could just barely hear it.
"Speak *up,* please," said Horton. He put his ear near it.

"My friend," came the voice, "you're a *very* fine friend.
You've helped all us folks on this dust speck no end.
You've saved all our houses, our ceilings and floors.
You've saved all our churches and grocery stores."

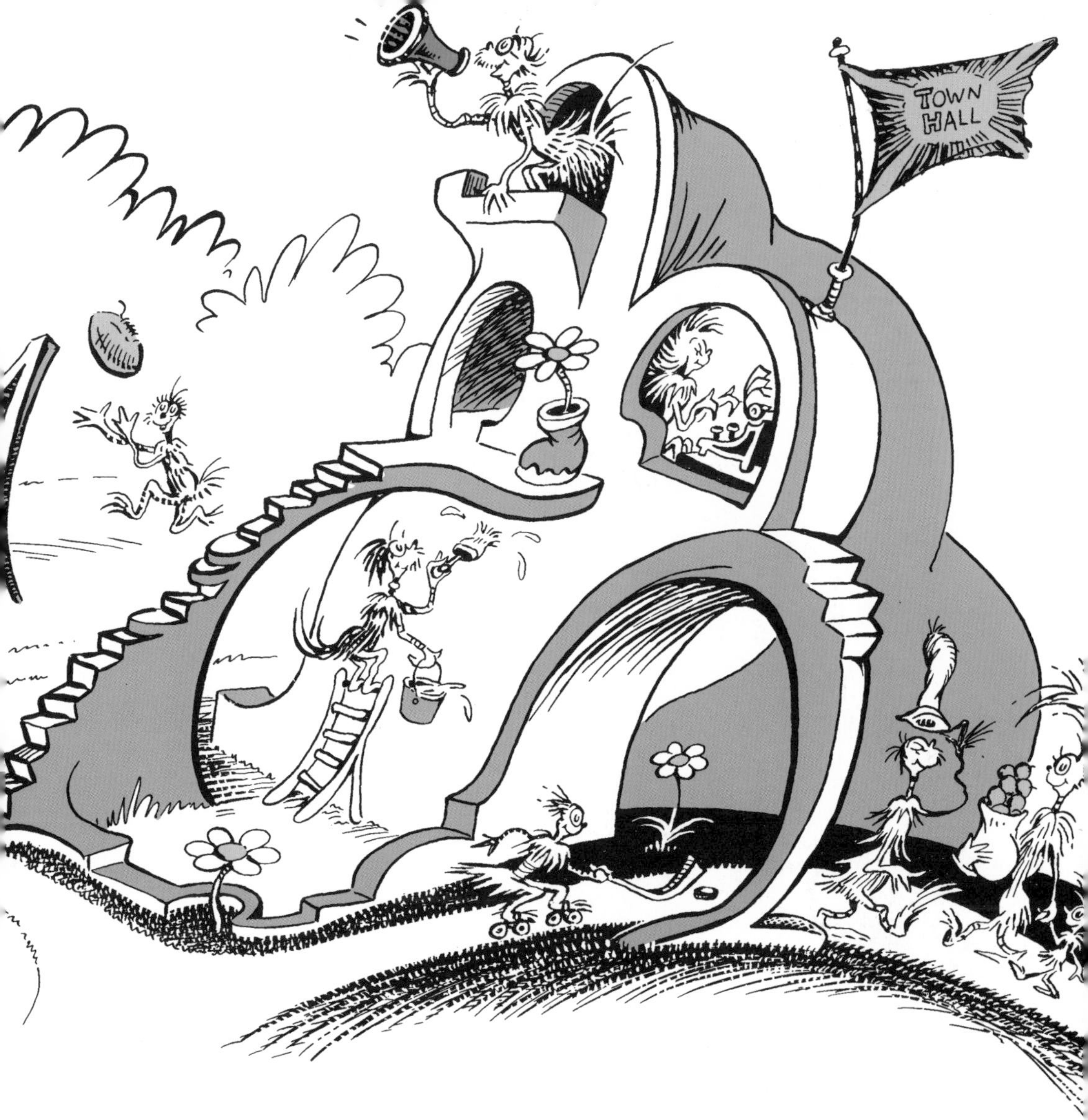

"You mean . . ." Horton gasped, "you have *buildings* there, *too?*"

"Oh, yes," piped the voice. "We most certainly do. . . .
"I know," called the voice, "I'm too small to be seen
But I'm Mayor of a town that is friendly and clean.
Our buildings, to you, would seem terribly small
But to us, who aren't big, they are wonderfully tall.
My town is called *Who*-ville, for I am a *Who*
And we *Whos* are all thankful and grateful to you."

And Horton called back to the Mayor of the town,
"You're safe now. Don't worry. I won't let you down."

But, just as he spoke to the Mayor of the speck,
Three big jungle monkeys climbed up Horton's neck!
The Wickersham Brothers came shouting, "What rot!
This elephant's talking to *Whos* who are *not!*
There *aren't* any *Whos!* And they *don't* have a Mayor!
And *we're* going to stop all this nonsense! *So there!"*

They snatched Horton's clover! They carried it off
To a black-bottomed eagle named Vlad Vlad-i-koff,
A mighty strong eagle, of very swift wing,
And they said, "Will you kindly get rid of this thing?"
And, before the poor elephant even could speak,
That eagle flew off with the flower in his beak.

All that late afternoon and far into the night
That black-bottomed bird flapped his wings in fast flight,
While Horton chased after, with groans, over stones
That tattered his toenails and battered his bones,
And begged, "Please don't harm all my little folks, who
Have as much right to live as us bigger folks do!"

But far, far beyond him, that eagle kept flapping
And over his shoulder called back, "Quit your yapping.
I'll fly the night through. I'm a bird. I don't mind it.
And I'll hide this, tomorrow, where *you'll* never find it!"

And at 6:56 the next morning he did it.
It sure was a terrible place that he hid it.
He let that small clover drop somewhere inside
Of a great patch of clovers a hundred miles wide!
"Find THAT!" sneered the bird. "But I think you will fail."
And he left
With a flip
Of his black-bottomed tail.

"I'll find it!" cried Horton. "I'll find it or bust!
I SHALL find my friends on my small speck of dust!"
And clover, by clover, by clover with care
He picked up and searched them, and called, "Are you there?"
But clover, by clover, by clover he found
That the one that he sought for was just not around.
And by noon poor old Horton, more dead than alive,
Had picked, searched, and piled up, nine thousand and five.

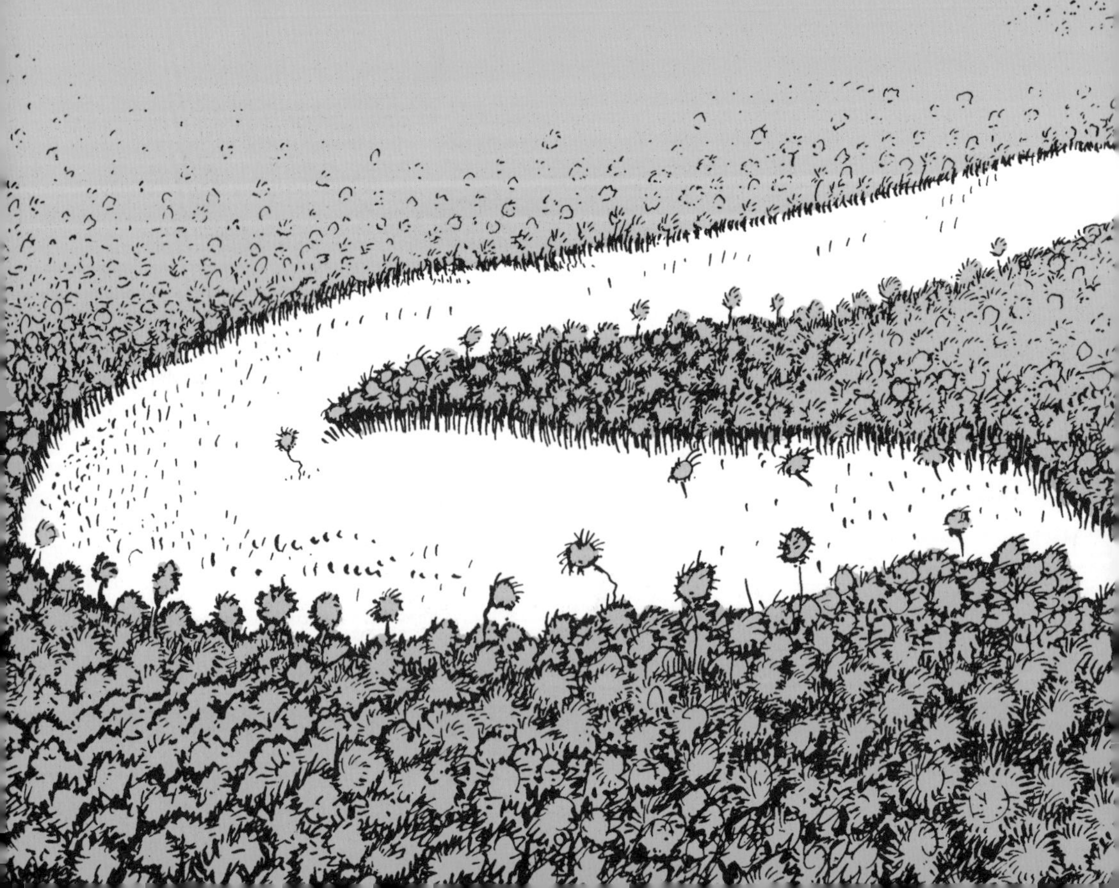

Then, on through the afternoon, hour after hour . . .
Till he found them at last! On the three millionth flower!
"My friends!" cried the elephant. "Tell me! Do tell!
Are you safe? Are you sound? Are you whole? Are you well?"

From down on the speck came the voice of the Mayor:

"We've *really* had trouble! Much more than our share.
When that black-bottomed birdie let go and we dropped,
We landed so hard that our clocks have all stopped.
Our tea-pots are broken. Our rocking-chairs smashed.
And our bicycle tyres all blew up when we crashed.
So, Horton, *please!*" pleaded that voice of the Mayor's,
"Will you stick by us *Whos* while we're making repairs?"

"Of course," Horton answered. "Of course I will stick.
I'll stick by you small folks through thin and through thick!"

"Humpf!"
Humpfed a voice!
"For almost two days you've run wild and insisted
On chatting with persons who've never existed.
Such carryings-on in our peaceable jungle!
We've had quite enough of your bellowing bungle!
And I'm here to state," snapped the big kangaroo,
"That your silly nonsensical game is all through!"
And the young kangaroo in her pouch said, "Me, too!"

"With the help of the Wickersham Brothers and dozens
Of Wickersham Uncles and Wickersham Cousins
And Wickersham In-Laws, whose help I've engaged,
You're going to be roped! And you're going to be caged!
And, as for your dust speck . . . *hah! That* we shall boil
In a hot steaming kettle of Beezle-Nut oil!"

"*Boil* it? . . ." gasped Horton!
"Oh, that you *can't* do!
It's all full of persons!
They'll *prove* it to you!"

"Mr. Mayor! Mr. Mayor!" Horton called. "Mr. Mayor!
You've *got* to prove now that you really are there!
So call a big meeting. Get everyone out.
Make every *Who* holler! Make every *Who* shout!
Make every *Who* scream! If you don't, every *Who*
Is going to end up in a Beezle-Nut stew!"

And, down on the dust speck, the scared little Mayor
Quick called a big meeting in *Who*-ville Town Square.
And his people cried loudly. They cried out in fear:
"We are here! We are here! We are here! We are here!"

The elephant smiled: "That was clear as a bell.
You kangaroos surely heard *that* very well."
"All I heard," snapped the big kangaroo, "was the breeze,
And the faint sound of wind through the far-distant trees.
I heard no small voices. And you didn't either."
And the young kangaroo in her pouch said, "Me, neither."

"Grab him!" they shouted. "And cage the big dope!
Lasso his stomach with ten miles of rope!
Tie the knots tight so he'll *never* shake loose!
Then dunk that dumb speck in the Beezle-Nut juice!"

Horton fought back with great vigour and vim
But the Wickersham gang was too many for him.
They beat him! They mauled him! They started to haul
Him into his cage! But he managed to call
To the Mayor: "Don't give up! I believe in you all!
A person's a person, no matter how small!
And you very small persons will *not* have to die
If you make yourselves heard! *So come on, now, and TRY!"*

The Mayor grabbed a tom-tom. He started to smack it.
And, all over *Who*-ville, they whooped up a racket.
They rattled tin kettles! They beat on brass pans,
On garbage pail tops and old cranberry cans!
They blew on bazookas and blasted great toots
On clarinets, oom-pahs and boom-pahs and flutes!

Great gusts of loud racket rang high through the air.
They rattled and shook the whole sky! And the Mayor
Called up through the howling mad hullabaloo:
"Hey, Horton! *How's this?* Is our sound coming through?"

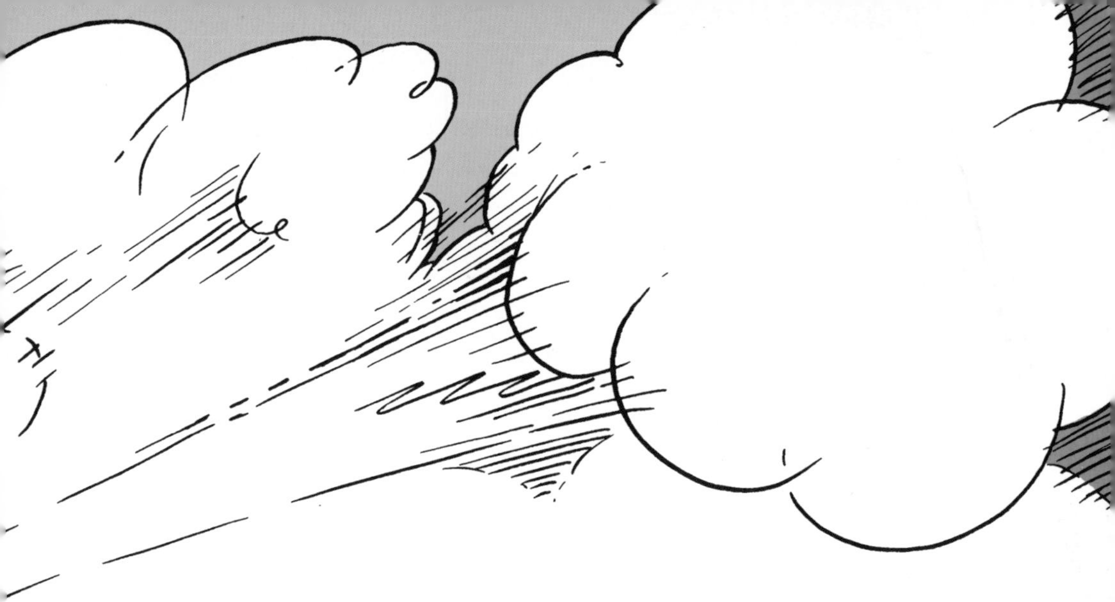

And Horton called back, "I can hear you just fine.
But the kangaroos' ears aren't as strong, quite, as mine.
They don't hear a thing! Are you *sure* all your boys
Are doing their best? Are they ALL making noise?
Are you sure every *Who* down in *Who*-ville is working?
Quick! Look through your town! Is there anyone shirking?"

Through the town rushed the Mayor, from the east to the west.
But *every*one seemed to be doing his best.
*Every*one seemed to be yapping or yipping!
*Every*one seemed to be beeping or bipping!
But it *wasn't enough,* all this ruckus and roar!
He HAD to find someone to help him make more.
He raced through each building! He searched floor-to-floor!

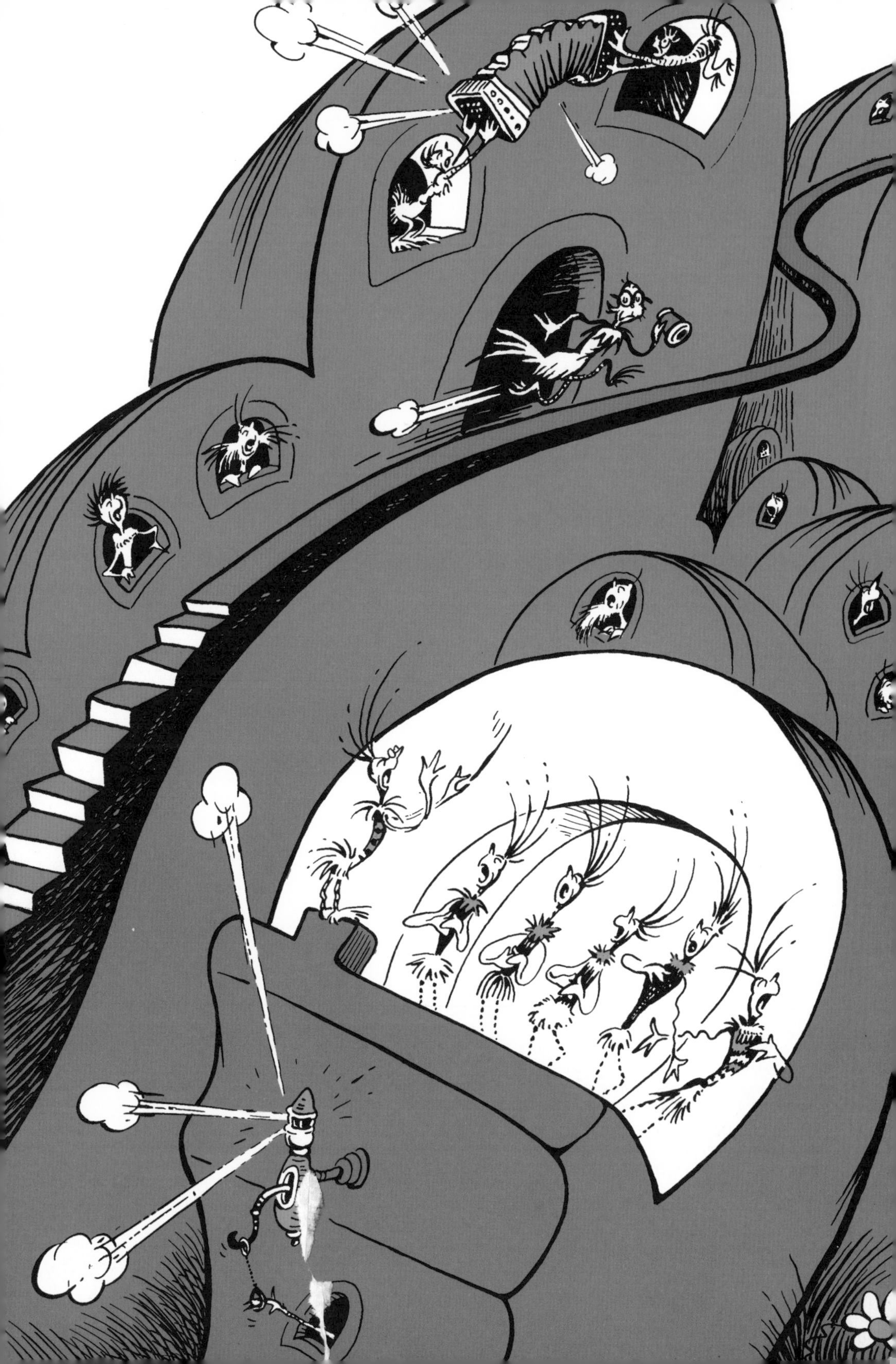

And, just as he felt he was getting nowhere,
And almost about to give up in despair,
He suddenly burst through a door and that Mayor
Discovered one shirker! Quite hidden away
In the Fairfax Apartments (Apartment 12-J)
A very small, *very* small shirker named Jo-Jo
Was standing, just standing, and bouncing a Yo-Yo!
Not making a sound! Not a yipp! Not a chirp!
And the Mayor rushed inside and he grabbed the young twerp!

APT.
12-J

And he climbed with the lad up the Eiffelberg Tower.

"This," cried the Mayor, "is your town's darkest hour!
The time for all *Whos* who have blood that is red
To come to the aid of their country!" he said.
"We've GOT to make noises in greater amounts!
So, open your mouth, lad! For every voice counts!"

Thus he spoke as he climbed. When they got to the top,
The lad cleared his throat and he shouted out, "YOPP!"

And that Yopp . . .
That one small, extra Yopp put it over!
Finally, at last! From that speck on that clover
Their voices were heard! They rang out clear and clean.
And the elephant smiled. "Do you see what I mean? . . .
They've proved they ARE persons, no matter how small.
And their whole world was saved by the Smallest of All!"

"How true! Yes, how true," said the big kangaroo.
"And, from now on, you know what I'm planning to do? . . .
From now on, I'm going to protect them with you!"
And the young kangaroo in her pouch said, . . .

"... ME, TOO!
From sun in the summer. From rain when it's fall-ish,
I'm going to protect them. No matter how small-ish!"

Yertle the Turtle and Other Stories

This Book is for
The Bartletts of Norwich, Vt.
and for
The Sagmasters of Cincinnati, Ohio

YERTLE the TURTLE

On the far-away Island of Sala-ma-Sond,
Yertle the Turtle was king of the pond.
A nice little pond. It was clean. It was neat.
The water was warm. There was plenty to eat
The turtles had everything turtles might need.
And they were all happy. Quite happy indeed.

They *were* . . . until Yertle, the king of them all,
Decided the kingdom he ruled was too small.
"I'm ruler," said Yertle, "of all that I see.
But I don't see *enough*. That's the trouble with me.
With this stone for a throne, I look down on my pond
But I cannot look down on the places beyond.
This throne that I sit on is too, too low down.
It ought to be *higher*!" he said with a frown.
"If I could sit high, how much greater I'd be!
What a king! I'd be ruler of all I could see!"

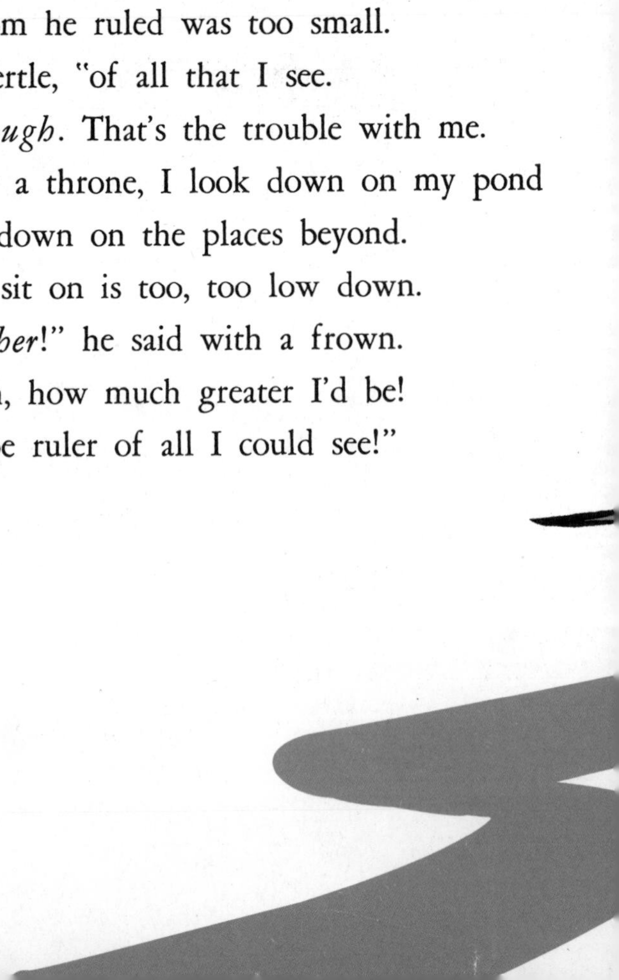

So Yertle, the Turtle King, lifted his hand
And Yertle, the Turtle King, gave a command.
He ordered nine turtles to swim to his stone
And, using these turtles, he built a *new* throne.
He made each turtle stand on another one's back
And he piled them all up in a nine-turtle stack.
And then Yertle climbed up. He sat down on the pile.
What a wonderful view! He could see 'most a mile!

"All mine!" Yertle cried. "Oh, the things I now rule!
I'm king of a cow! And I'm king of a mule!
I'm king of a house! And, what's more, beyond that,
I'm king of a blueberry bush and a cat!
I'm Yertle the Turtle! Oh, marvellous me!
For I am the ruler of all that I see!"

And all through that morning, he sat there up high
Saying over and over, "A great king am I!"
Until round about noon. Then he heard a faint sigh.
"What's *that?*" snapped the king
And he looked down the stack.
And he saw, at the bottom, a turtle named Mack.
Just a part of his throne. And this plain little turtle
Looked up and he said, "Beg your pardon, King Yertle.
"I've pains in my back and my shoulders and knees.
How long must we stand here, Your Majesty, please?"

"SILENCE!" the King of the Turtles barked back.
"I'm king, and you're only a turtle named Mack."

"You stay in your place while I sit here and rule.
I'm king of a cow! And I'm king of a mule!
I'm king of a house! And a bush! And a cat!
But that isn't all. I'll do better than *that*!
My throne shall be *higher*!" his royal voice thundered,
"So pile up more turtles! I want 'bout two hundred!"

"Turtles! More turtles!" he bellowed and brayed.
And the turtles 'way down in the pond were afraid.
They trembled. They shook. But they came. They obeyed.
From all over the pond, they came swimming by dozens.
Whole families of turtles, with uncles and cousins.
And all of them stepped on the head of poor Mack.
One after another, they climbed up the stack.

THEN Yertle the Turtle was perched up so high,
He could see forty miles from his throne in the sky!
"Hooray!" shouted Yertle. "I'm king of the trees!
I'm king of the birds! And I'm king of the bees!
I'm king of the butterflies! King of the air!
Ah, me! What a throne! What a wonderful chair!
I'm Yertle the Turtle! Oh, marvellous me!
For I am the ruler of all that I see!"

Then again, from below, in the great heavy stack,
Came a groan from that plain little turtle named Mack.
"Your Majesty, please . . . I don't like to complain,
But down here below, we are feeling great pain.
I know, up on top you are seeing great sights,
But down at the bottom we, too, should have rights.
We turtles can't stand it. Our shells will all crack!
Besides, we need food. We are starving!" groaned Mack.

"You hush up your mouth!" howled the mighty King Yertle.
"You've no right to talk to the world's highest turtle.
I rule from the clouds! Over land! Over sea!
There's nothing, no, NOTHING, that's higher than me!"

But, while he was shouting, he saw with surprise
That the moon of the evening was starting to rise
Up over his head in the darkening skies.
"What's THAT?" snorted Yertle. "What IS that thing
That dares to be higher than Yertle the King?
I shall not allow it! I'll go higher still!
I'll build my throne higher! I can and I will!
I'll call some more turtles. I'll stack 'em to heaven!
I need 'bout five thousand, six hundred and seven!"

BURP!

But, as Yertle, the Turtle King, lifted his hand
And started to order and give the command,
That plain little turtle below in the stack,
That plain little turtle whose name was just Mack,
Decided he'd taken enough. And he had.
And that plain little lad got a little bit mad
And that plain little Mack did a plain little thing.
He burped!
And his burp shook the throne of the king!

And Yertle the Turtle, the king of the trees,
The king of the air and the birds and the bees,
The king of a house and a cow and a mule...
Well, *that* was the end of the Turtle King's rule!
For Yertle, the King of all Sala-ma-Sond,
Fell off his high throne and fell *Plunk*! in the pond!

And today the great Yertle, that Marvellous he,
Is King of the Mud. That is all he can see.
And the turtles, of course . . . all the turtles are free
As turtles and, maybe, all creatures should be.

Gertrude McFuzz

There once was a girl-bird named Gertrude McFuzz
And she had the smallest plain tail ever was.
One droopy-droop feather. That's all that she had.
And, oh! That one feather made Gertrude so sad.

For there was another young bird that she knew,
A fancy young birdie named Lolla-Lee-Lou,
And instead of *one* feather behind, she had *two*!
Poor Gertrude! Whenever she happened to spy
Miss Lolla-Lee-Lou flying by in the sky,
She got very jealous. She frowned. And she pouted.
Then, one day she got awfully cross and she shouted:
"This just isn't fair! I have *one*! She has *two*!
I MUST have a tail just like Lolla-Lee-Lou!"

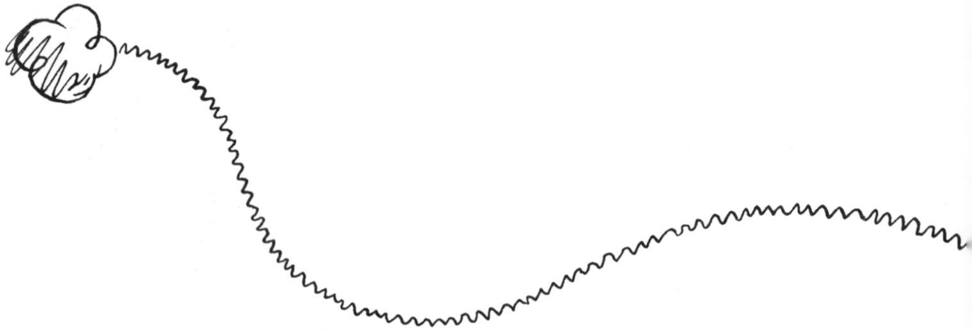

So she flew to her uncle, a doctor named Dake
Whose office was high in a tree by the lake
And she cried, "Uncle Doctor! Oh, please do you know
Of some kind of a pill that will make my tail grow?"
"Tut tut!" said the doctor. "Such talk! How absurd!
Your tail is just right for your kind of a bird."

Then Gertrude had tantrums. She raised such a din
That finally her uncle, the doctor, gave in
And he told her just where she could find such a pill
On a pill-berry vine on the top of the hill.
"Oh, thank you!" chirped Gertrude McFuzz, and she flew
Right straight to the hill where the pill-berry grew.

Yes! There was the vine! And as soon as she saw it
She plucked off a berry. She started to gnaw it.
It tasted just awful. Almost made her sick.
But she wanted that tail, so she swallowed it quick.
Then she felt something happen! She felt a small twitch
As if she'd been tapped, down behind, by a switch.
And Gertrude looked 'round. And she cheered! It was true!
Two feathers! Exactly like Lolla-Lee-Lou!

Then she had an idea! "Now I know what I'll do...
I'll grow a tail *better* than Lolla-Lee-Lou!"

"These pills that grow feathers are working just fine!"
So she nibbled *another* one off of the vine!

She felt a *new* twitch. And then Gertrude yelled, "WHEE!
Miss Lolla has only just *two*! I have *three*!
When Lolla-Lee-Lou sees this beautiful stuff,
She'll fall right down flat on her face, sure enough!
I'll show HER who's pretty! I certainly will!
Why, I'll make my tail even prettier still!"

She snatched at those berries that grew on that vine.
She gobbled down four, five, six, seven, eight, nine!
And she didn't stop eating, young Gertrude McFuzz,
Till she'd eaten three dozen! That's all that there was.

Then the feathers popped out! With a *zang*! With a *zing*!
They blossomed like flowers that bloom in the spring.
All fit for a queen! What a sight to behold!
They sparkled like diamonds and gumdrops and gold!
Like silk! Like spaghetti! Like satin! Like lace!
They burst out like rockets all over the place!
They waved in the air and they swished in the breeze!
And some were as long as the branches of trees.
And *still* they kept growing! They popped and they popped
Until, round about sundown when, finally, they stopped.

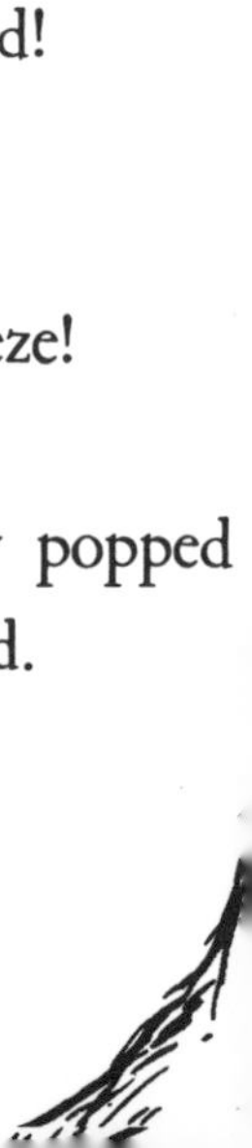

"And NOW," giggled Gertrude, "The next thing to do
Is to fly right straight home and show Lolla-Lee-Lou!
And when Lolla sees *these*, why her face will get red
And she'll let out a scream and she'll fall right down dead!"

Then she spread out her wings to take off from the ground,
But, with all of those feathers, she weighed ninety pound!
She yanked and she pulled and she let out a squawk,
But that bird couldn't fly! Couldn't run! Couldn't walk!

And all through that night, she was stuck on that hill,
And Gertrude McFuzz might be stuck up there still
If her good Uncle Dake hadn't heard the girl yelp.
He rushed to her rescue and brought along help.

To lift Gertrude up almost broke all their beaks
And to fly her back home, it took almost two weeks.
And *then* it took almost another week more
To pull out those feathers. My! Gertrude was sore!

And, finally, when all of the pulling was done,
Gertrude, behind her, again had just one...
That one little feather she had as a starter.
But now that's enough, because now she is smarter.

EXTRA MOOSE MOSS
for HELEN

THIDWICK the Big-Hearted MOOSE

By Dr. Seuss

Up at Lake Winna-Bango . . . the far northern shore . . .
Lives a huge herd of moose, about sixty or more,
And they all go around in a big happy bunch
Looking for nice tender moose-moss to munch.

Up at Lake Winna-Bango, one day, they were lunching,
Just strolling along and enjoying their munching . . .
(For the moose-moss that day was especially fine) . . .
When it happened that Thidwick, the last moose in line,
Saw a Bingle Bug sitting.
The bug called out, "Hey!
It's *such* a long road
And it's *such* a hot day,
Would you mind if I rode
On your horns for a way?"

"Of course not!" smiled Thidwick, the Big-Hearted Moose.
"I'm happy my antlers can be of some use.
There's room there to spare, and I'm happy to share!
Be my guest and I hope that you're comfortable there!"

So the Bingle Bug picked out a nice easy seat
And the moose went on looking for moose-moss to eat.

Well . . .
An hour or so later
The bug heard a squeak,
And he heard the small voice
Of a Tree-Spider speak.
"I say!" said the spider,
"You've got a fine place!
That moose seems quite friendly,
Has such a nice face . . .
If I got on, *too,*
Do you think he would mind . . . ?"

"Hop aboard!" laughed the bug. "And I think that you'll find
That the moose won't object. He's the big-hearted kind!"

"I accept," said the spider,
"With joy and delight."
And he started a web
On the horn to the right.

While the spider was spinning, he heard a gay song
And a fresh little Zinn-a-zu Bird came along.
He stopped. And he stared. And he chirped, "Well! *Well!* WELL!
What a smart place to build! What a great place to dwell!
I've been living on *trees* ever since I was born,
But here's something *new!* Why not live on a *horn!*
If there's room there for two, then there's room there for three!"

"There's plenty of room!"
Laughed the bug. "And it's free!"

Thidwick stopped walking.
What *was* all that talking?
These guests had caught Thidwick the Moose unawares.
"Hey!" he called out. *"What goes on there upstairs?"*

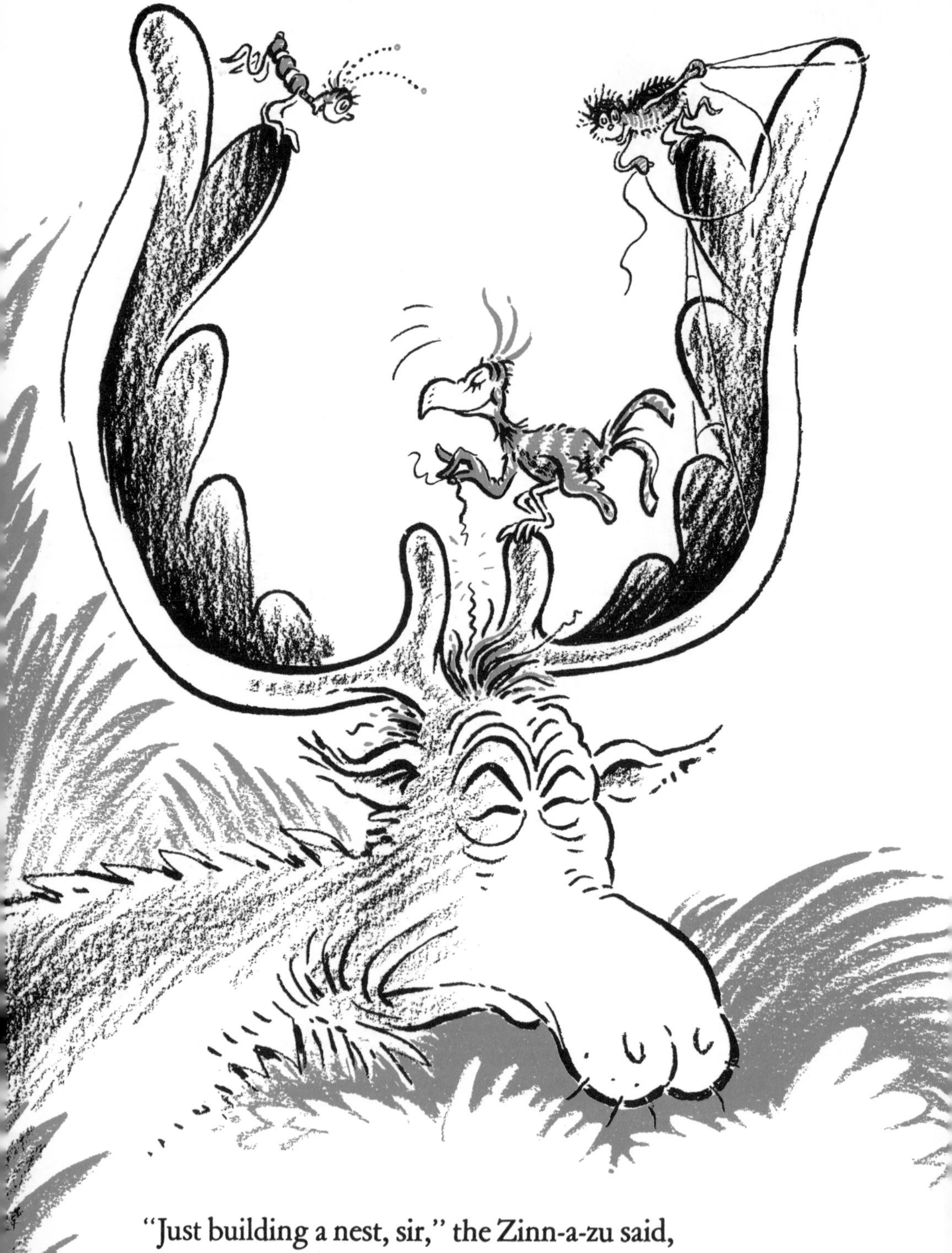

"Just building a nest, sir," the Zinn-a-zu said,
And began yanking hairs out of poor Thidwick's head.
And he plucked out exactly two hundred and four!
"Don't worry," he laughed. "You can always grow more!"

Then he dozed off to sleep in his fine moose-hair nest.
"This bird," murmured Thidwick, "is sort of a pest!
But I'm a good sport, so I'll just let him rest,
For a host, above all, must be nice to his guest."

"Besides, now, it's getting quite late in the day
And *surely* tomorrow they'll all go away."

But, alas! The next morning
The sun's early light
Brought to Thidwick's sad eyes
A most *un*welcome sight. . . .

"Meet my wife!" said the bird.
"I was married last night.

"And, perhaps; by the way,
I should mention to you
That her uncle is coming
To live with us, too.
You're a very fine host
So I knew you'd be willing . . ."

Then the Uncle, a Woodpecker,
Started in drilling!

All Thidwick's friends shouted, "GET RID OF THOSE PESTS!"
"I would, but I can't," sobbed poor Thidwick. *"They're guests!"*

"Guests indeed!" his friends answered, and all of them frowned.
"If *those* are your guests, we don't want *you* around!
You can't stay with us, 'cause you're just not our sort!"
And they all turned their backs and walked off with a snort.

Now the big friendless moose walked alone and forlorn,
With four great big woodpecker holes in his horn.

"What holes!" whispered Herman, a squirrel, who spied 'em.
"What holes to hide nuts in! *Hmmm!* Mind if I tried 'em?"

"They're yours!" called the woodpecker. "Get right inside 'em!
This big-hearted moose runs a public hotel!
Bring your nuts! Bring your wife! Bring your children as well!"

So the whole squirrel family all jumped on, pell mell.

And the very next thing the poor animal knew,
A Bobcat and Turtle were living there, too!
NOW what was the big-hearted moose going to do?

Well, what would YOU do
If it happened to YOU?

You couldn't say "Skat!" 'cause that wouldn't be right.
You couldn't shout "Scram!" 'cause that isn't polite.
A host has to put up with all kinds of pests,
For a host, above all, must be nice to his guests.
So you'd try hard to smile, and you'd try to look sweet
And you'd go right on looking for moose-moss to eat.

But now it was winter and *that* wasn't easy,
For moose-moss gets scarce when the weather gets freezy.
The food was soon gone on the cold northern shore
Of Lake Winna-Bango. There just was no more!
And all Thidwick's friends swam away in a bunch
To the south of the lake where there's moose-moss to munch.

He watched the herd leaving. And then Thidwick knew
He'd starve if he stayed here! He'd have to go, too!

He stepped in the water. Then, oh! what a fuss!
"STOP!" screamed his guests. "You can't do this to us!
These horns are our home and you've no right to take
Our home to the far distant side of the lake!"

"Be fair!" Thidwick begged, with a lump in his throat. . . .

"We're fair," said the bug.
"We'll decide this by vote.
All those in favour of going, say 'AYE,'
All those in favour of staying, say 'NAY'."

"AYE!" shouted Thidwick,
But when he was done...

"NAY!" they all yelled.
He lost 'leven to one.

"We win!" screamed the guests, "by a very large score!"
And poor, starving Thidwick climbed back on the shore.
Then, do you know what those pests did?
They asked in some more!

They asked in a fox, who jumped in from the trees,
They asked in some mice and they asked in some fleas.
They asked a big bear in and then, if you please,
Came a swarm of three hundred and sixty-two bees!

Poor Thidwick sank down, with a groan, to his knees.
And *then,* THEN came something thatmade his heart freeze .

Bullets came zinging right past Thidwick's face!
Guns were bang-binging all over the place!

"Get that moose!
Get that moose!"
Thidwick heard a voice call.
"Fire again and again
And shoot straight, one and all!
We *must* get his head
For the Harvard Club wall!"

Thidwick took to his heels with that load on his head!
With five hundred pounds on his horns, the moose fled!
He could have run faster without all those pests,
But a host, above all, must be nice to his guests.

Up canyon! Off cliff! Over wild rocky trail!
With bullets bang-bouncing around him like hail!
Up gully! Through gulch! And down slippery sluice,
With his hard-hearted guests raced the soft-hearted moose!

Then finally they had him!

Because of those pests, he had run out of luck,
Because of those guests on his horns, he was stuck!

He gasped! He felt faint! And the whole world grew fuzzy!
Thidwick was finished, completely. . . .

. . . or WAS he . . . ?

Finished . . . ?
Not Thidwick!
DECIDEDLY NOT!
It's true, he was in a most terrible spot,
But NOW he remembered a thing he'd forgot!
A wonderful something that happens each year
To the horns of all moose and the horns of all deer.

Today was the day,
Thidwick happened to know . . .

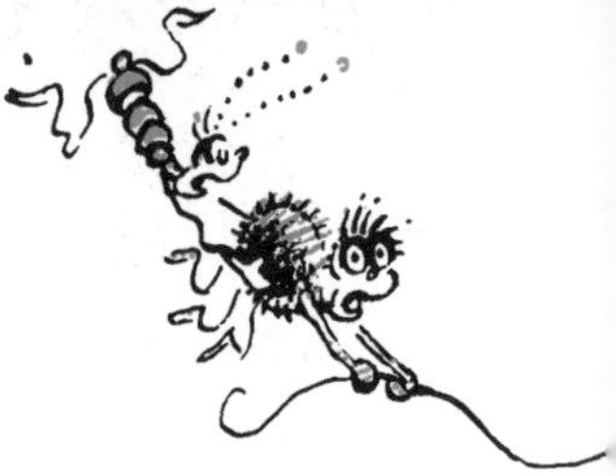

. . . that OLD horns come off so that NEW ones can grow!

And he called to the pests on his horns as he threw 'em,
"You wanted my horns; now you're quite welcome to 'em!
Keep 'em! They're yours!
As for ME, I shall take
Myself to the far distant
Side of the lake!"

And he swam Winna-Bango and found his old bunch,
And arrived just in time for a wonderful lunch
At the south of the lake, where there's moose-moss to munch.

His *old* horns today are
Where *you* knew they *would* be.
His guests are still on them,
All stuffed, as they *should* be.